♦ The Menagerie ♦

a fairy tale (with asides)

by Mason Ball

Illustrated by Jon Attfield

Text copyright © 2015 by Mason Ball
Illustrations copyright © 2015 by Jon Attfield

All rights reserved. This book or any portion thereof may not be reproduced or used in any manner whatsoever without the express written permission of the publisher except for the use of brief quotations in a book review.

Printed in the United Kingdom

First Printing, 2015

ISBN 978-1-326-28449-7

www.benjaminlouche.com
www.thedoublerclub.co.uk

Author's Note

The main body of *The Menagerie* arrived almost fully formed one night in that strange hypnagogic state between sleep and waking; though it was not without its catalyst.

After years of planning to do so, I finally got around to reading a collection of original Grimm's fairytales; in fact (and purely on request I assure you), I took to reading them aloud to my wife before we went to sleep. This can have had nothing if not a profound influence on my mind the night that *The Menagerie* made its appearance.

Much is made of the dark nature of Jacob and Wilhelm's tales, but little, I think, of just how genuinely strange and, for want of a better term, 'thematically asymmetrical' they are. Often the accepted beginning-middle-end structure we're so used to is utterly discarded, sometimes it seems merely in the pure, unadulterated joy of the telling of the tale.

That strangeness, coupled with the fairy tale's traditional yet slightly 'off' use of language, the repetition of phrases, the often almost clumsily formal syntax (perhaps due to wonky translation of the original?) adds a certain dreamlike quality to the tale and makes, particularly for an adult reader, a very odd yet enjoyable experience.

I will hint at no further specifics concerning the Grimm's strangeness but instead simply implore you to find a copy and read them.

What follows is the result of my tired brain infused with The Grimm's magic, oddity and tragedy.

You may choose to read this book by flitting back and forth between the story and the notes, or 'asides', at the back (and if this is the methodology you choose, might I suggest investing in a second bookmark?), or you may choose to save the notes until after the meat of the story has had its moment, told its truths, and only then to digest them.

Mason Ball

Contents

The Menagerie 11
Several Asides 87

List of Illustrations

A gift 9
"And they wandered" 15
"Climb aboard" 21
"An immense tent was being raised" 27
The Clown / The Singer 31
The Geek / The Aerialists 35
The Lion Tamer / The Juggler 39
The HeShe / The Fire Eater 43
"The lion pounced" 49
"Two grey birds" 53
"Headlong and alone into the dark" 59
"Another tripwire, then another" 63
"Night fell and the interior of the wagon darkened" 67
"Small piles of feathers" 71
"A living thunderhead" 77
"An unending torrent of black birds" 81
End 85

♦ The Menagerie ♦

The Children

They were two specks on a road that stretched on and on, unhindered, through a yawning, dusty plain.

They made a play at walking somewhere, when in fact all they were doing was wandering, hungry, and not a little lost. The girl had long, brown hair and the boy a tough, stony look in his eye. They were brother and sister, he a year older than she, and just about a hand taller.

They measured horses in hands, their mother had told them, but neither the girl nor the boy had seen a horse in as long as they could remember; no one had. Nor, for that matter, had they seen their mother for weeks, perhaps months. She had gone out for food, telling them to lock the door, telling the boy to look after his sister, and never returned.

The air through which they wandered was hot and damp and the same bile yellow it had been since that first morning after what had happened had happened, not that they could recall it, but they had been told.[1]

People had withdrawn from the world after it happened, locked their doors and watched from windows. Houses had become forts. Animal traps littered lawns, tripwires festooned picket fences and paths; snares caught the curious and hungry, who were left to expire on brown, brittle grass. Shotguns were taken down from walls, cleaned and loaded. Shots popped and cracked in the night like clandestine fireworks. Everyone guarded their own little square of earth.

Dogs roamed, bared their teeth and showed their ribs; yet in time even dogs vanished, eaten. Birds too. People too, some said.

All the children knew of this was that their mother had told them not to wander and not to answer the door to anyone but her; she had told them not to wander and yet this is exactly what they had done. They passed people on the road from time to time but seldom spoke. The frightened travellers eyed one another suspiciously and passed on by.

The girl held the boy's pocketknife, a gift, given with their mother's parting words in mind. The boy held a corkscrew, a little too tightly, as if unsure of its use should things take a dark turn.

The Caravan

When they had been walking for a week or more, a strange dotted line appeared on the horizon, like an army of ants marching single file, tracing some forgotten picnic perhaps, or trail of blood. In time, the ants revealed themselves to be a caravan of painted wagons rocking and trundling across the plain, lead by tired, threadbare horses, crossing the road at a right angle and continuing on as if the road itself were nothing but a nonsensical scratch in the sand, a discarded ribbon, and of no more meaning nor purpose.

When close enough, the children stopped, and squinting into the sun, watched.

The paint on the wagons had once been bright and vivid but time had dulled them, dried and cracked their lettering, their frescoes of strange figures with painted faces, of dancing animals, of men and of women in glorious costume performing incredible and impossible feats: flying, tumbling, riding plumed ponies.

The girl was the first to notice that on every wagon hung a collection of metal cages, a single bird in each, sometimes as many as six cages to a wagon; the birds were all of different shapes, sizes and colours. They squawked and tweeted, ruffled their feathers and nodded on their perches as the wagons swung and lolled on worn wheels. It was the first either of the children had heard birdsong in weeks and despite their ragged clothes, their grumbling stomachs, it made them smile. They gawped at the wonder, at the reality of the birds, and of the horses.

As the last wagon in the caravan passed them, the man driving it pulled hard on the reins, drawing it to a stop. He surveyed the children awhile from up in his seat, glanced once around him at the emptiness, put on a tall black hat which held three yellow feathers[2], and jumped down.

"You're lost," he said. It wasn't a question. The boy bristled a little, stepped in front of his sister, the corkscrew held behind his back.

"We're *fine*," he said, full of bravado. The man in the tall hat looked them over.

"You don't look so fine," he said, "you look hungry. You look young."

"We're fine," said the boy again.

"Well," said the man, then, to the girl, "can you sew, young lady?" The girl nodded that she could. "You don't mind raw fingers, we got sewing needs doing, got food needs eating. You both got bellies need filling."

"We're fine," said the boy again.

"You said that already." The man spat, turned around, looked about them. "I seen a pack of wild dogs yonder," he pointed in the direction the children had been walking, "you best be careful."

"There ain't any dogs," said the boy.

"No, and there ain't any horses nor birds neither," replied the man, "yet here we are."

"I can sew," said the girl.

"Climb aboard, we'll keep you both safe." The boy and the girl looked at one another for a long time. All about them the country opened its mouth to swallow them. The man in the tall hat climbed back up to his seat on the wagon. The girl nodded to her brother and his shoulders sank a little.

The Wagon

They rode, rattling about in the back of the man's wagon, among boxes and bundles, barrels and blankets, for hours. Darkness fell. The girl slept, happy to be off of her feet; the boy fought to stay awake, glaring at the back of the man's head as he drove, lest he turn into a wild animal, or a carnivorous phantom, and crawl back to devour them; but in the end, the boy too succumbed to sleep.

The Company (in part)

When the girl woke it was light again and the sound of many voices, of movement, drew her from the wagon and out into the day. People were everywhere, to-ing and fro-ing, carrying heavy looking boxes or long swathes of canvas; large metal stakes were being driven into the earth by men wielding huge hammers. An immense tent was being raised. Wherever someone worked, beside them sat a birdcage, and in that cage, sat a bird. It became clear to the girl that every cage they had seen belonged to a single person and as she watched them work, it became clear that every person took their bird with them wherever they went.

The man in the tall hat approached her, carrying his own cage, inside it a black bird with a vividly orange beak and yellow markings about its eyes. The bird looked at the girl with an eye like a polished marble, its head jerking strangely; it whistled a single, long note and looked at her again, this time with the other eye.

"Who are you all?" asked the girl, "where are we?"

"We're wherever we ended up," said the man in the tall hat.

"What's that tent for?"

"We are entertainers and such," said the man, "we travel about. We are The Menagerie. We stage spectacles. Every so often we'll pick up wanderers. We'll keep you safe."

"Keep you safe!" said the bird, "We'll keep you! We'll keep you! We'll keep you safe!"

"You're an entertainer," said the girl, still woozy from sleep, trying to understand.

"Me? O, I'm what you might call the mouthpiece, ringmaster, a mere hyperbolic bloviator." The girl began to wonder who might leave the safety of their homes to make up the audience for such an entertainment.

"Do many people come along?"

"O, sometimes they do. We go on regardless. We travel on, we never turn back. It's what we do." The girl thought what a queer sight it must be, a show without an audience; she thought distantly of something she'd heard once, about a tree falling in the woods and not making a sound.

In truth, The Ringmaster[3] could not recall the last time the performers had had an audience, but he did not tell the girl this.

He pointed out some of the others as they passed. "That's The Juggler," he said as a well-dressed man walked by carrying a large cage holding a magpie. "That's The Singer," he said as a tall, striking woman passed by carrying a cage holding a small, bright scarlet bird with black wings. "That's The Lion Tamer," he said as an angry looking woman walked by, throwing a sour look at the girl; in her cage sat a dark and olive green bird with a white patch under its beak and black spray of feathers poking up from its head.

"You have a lion?!" asked the girl, open mouthed, amazed at the very idea.

"Of course," he said, and smiled, "A lion tamer wouldn't be very much use without one, would it?"

"And it's peaceful here? Not like out there?" she gestured back the way they had come.

"It is," he replied proudly, adding strangely "we have our birds and we are safe."

When The Ringmaster had left to help in the preparations, the boy, who had been watching everything and listening intently, climbed from the wagon and joined his sister.

"His bird is a Myna bird, I remember from my bird books. Myna birds can speak."

"I know," said the girl, "I heard it."

"What did it say?" asked the boy.

"That they will keep us safe." The boy nodded slowly and put the corkscrew back in his pocket.

"We'll see," he said.

The Spectacle

That night, inside the grand tent, as a jaundiced moon rose over the plain, and with only the boy and the girl as audience, the show began.

In the dimness, the buzz of a drum roll. Then, in the warmth and sweep of spotlights, motes of dust danced, the air tangible with music and expectation. As the musicians played, The Ringmaster appeared in an icy circle of light, booming his welcome to the empty seats. He spoke in long, extravagant words, made elaborate and hypnotic gestures with his cane, while in his other hand the Myna bird swung in its cage.

The Clown [4]

First into the ring was a figure dressed in enormous baggy clothing of bright, clashing colours, his face painted white, his nose a red ball, his eyes black crosses, his eyelids bright blue, his lips enormous and red; his shoes were comically huge. He hung his bird cage, inside a garish and impressive parrot, from the pole in the centre of the tent ("Scarlet Macaw," whispered the boy to his sister) and went into his act. He capered and fell, he tripped with measured clumsiness, he tumbled and he performed acts of acrobatic skill and daring, he stepped on rakes whose handles jumped up to hit him in the face, he threw buckets of confetti at the brother and sister; despite themselves, they giggled and clapped.

The Singer [5]

Oozing into the light in a beautiful red dress that sparkled and shone like rubies, the statuesque beauty hung her bird on a hook by the stage ("Scarlet Tanager," said the boy) and after a breath, launched into a song with a voice of such depth of feeling, of such dizzying variety, that the skin on the boy and the girl rose up in goosebumps and their eyes brimmed with tears.

The Geek [6]

    A chicken was thrown into the ring and began immediately to peck among the sawdust. Next there came a great rattling of chains and a half naked man with a shock of dirty matted hair atop his head, his skin smeared with filth, was loosed into the ring. He was as a wild beast and the girl drew back, grasping at her brother's hand, which in turn gripped hers with equal fright. The man wore about his neck an iron collar, a birdcage chained to it, so that it pulled him down into an animalistic stoop, swinging wildly as he ran about, throwing him off balance with every other step; the bird inside ("Gannet" said the boy) flapped and squawked. So long, thick and tangled was the man's hair, that all that could be seen of his face was his mouth, which was filled with uneven, rotten teeth. The man chased the chicken all about the place, while the musicians played comedic tunes and accented his every mistake or mishap with loud bursts or cymbal crashes. Eventually he caught the chicken, and the music rose to a crescendo. He forced the chicken's head into his mouth and as the girl looked away, the boy forced himself to watch as the man bit off its head and swallowed it down whole.

The Aerialists [7]

    Next, The Ringmaster commanded their attention upwards as two figures in bright jewel-encrusted costumes climbed rope ladders to the very top of the tent. They were a man and a woman, "Husband and wife!"

cried The Ringmaster, "Keepers of the greatest love that ever dared fall upon mortal man!" They carried one cage between them as they climbed, within it two bright green and orange birds ("Love Birds," came the whisper in the girl's ear). The cage was fastened to the central tent pole, the couple kissed, somewhat passionlessly thought the girl, and each climbed onto their own trapeze.

Back and forth they swung, dizzyingly high above the heads of the brother and sister, swapping trapezes, letting go their own and flying, truly *flying* it seemed, until they gripped the bar before them once again. Below, the boy and the girl held their breaths, then gasped aloud, then held their breaths again. Just then, some misjudgement was made and The Aerialists collided, both retaining their grip, yet their momentum had been interrupted and for a time they hung and twisted awkwardly. An argument broke out between them, even as they hung there, blame for the mishap thrown back and forth, though the exact words could not be heard by the children. Just then, the man slapped his wife across the face. She immediately slapped him back, though harder, and they lunged at one another, grabbing great fists of the other's costume. The Ringmaster quickly invited applause to signal the end of their act, though their final flourish had not been performed. They climbed down, furious and bickering, to the sound of the children's weak and uncomfortable clapping.

Interval

A thin, sad looking man, whose bird was a sparrow, came around to offer the boy and the girl peanuts, popcorn, candy floss or toffee apples.
"We don't have any money," the boy told him.
"Free of charge," said the man cheerfully. The boy whispered to his sister that they should politely refuse.
"I don't trust them," he said. But the girl told him that his worries made no sense. She said that had the people of The Menagerie wanted to harm them, they could have done so already, at any time, in any number of ways. She took a toffee apple and immediately bit into it.
"See?" she told her brother, "not poisoned." After that, the boy reluctantly accepted a bag of peanuts.

The Lion Tamer [8]

The lion prowled about its cage as the angry looking woman the girl had seen earlier cracked a large red whip and waved a dining chair at the beast. Her bird looked on ("Eastern Whipbird" said the boy, "see the plume atop its head?"). In time she coaxed the lion onto a large painted plinth and half with threat, half with cajoling, it balanced, first on its hind legs and then upon its forelegs, to which the brother and sister applauded wildly. The act ended with the angry looking woman placing her head into the lion's open mouth, so full of enormous, sharp teeth, and them retrieving her head unharmed, a practise the boy though foolish in the extreme and likely to end one day with her not having much of a head to speak of at all.

The Juggler [9]

    With the Ringmaster's cry of "Ladies and gentlemen, I give you now, the unparalleled and prestidigitatorial, the ambidexter extraordinary..." The well-dressed man appeared in a black tail coat, white shirt and white bow tie, looking for all the world like a lord or duke of some kind; his Magpie sat to one side as he performed. He proceeded to throw and catch a bewildering array of objects which he pulled from a large leather bag: balls, bells, knives, clubs, fruit, a china vase, all at once, eventually doing this while balancing a chair upon his forehead. Astonished, the girl imagined that perhaps the very air around him was somehow immune to gravity.

The HeShe [10]

Next, a beautiful woman came into the ring, however, when she turned around, she became a handsome man, then when she faced front, half was a man and half a woman. The man half had a moustache and wore a pinstripe suit and tie, the woman half had exquisite make up, a shock of red coiffured hair and a long, flowing ball gown. The boy thought it very funny that a man might wear a woman's clothing, or that a woman might wear a man's; the girl thought only of how magical it was that two people could exist in only one body.

In her/his hand hung a cage holding a brown bird, almost shockingly muted against his/her costume, with an extravagant curlicue of tail feathers ("Lyrebird," said the boy). A gramophone played and he/she mouthed the words to the song playing, as if the voice came from his/her body and not the gramophone. The result was strange and bewitching and the children applauded with great wonder and enthusiasm.

The Fire Eater [11]

Last came a slight woman in a resplendent leotard of gold, orange and red; she carried a cage over which was thrown a heavy black cloth and from which rose tendrils of thin smoke; from time to time a dull glow seemed to leak forth from inside. At no point in her act, or after, did she remove the cloth to reveal whatever strange bird lay within.

She proceeded to light torches on fire and run them across her bare skin, yet remained strangely, impossibly unburned! She extinguished the torches in her mouth only to light them again and extinguish them again, moving the fire hypnotically in the air before her. At any moment the children thought she would go up in flames herself. To end, she drew a torch to her lips and breathed out a long, fiercely bright, yellow torrent of fire into the air above her, its heat pushing the children back into their seats and filling their imaginations with all the impossibilities of the night, sending them to their beds with dreams the like of which they had never dreamed before.

The Clown & The Lion

Several days later, in another part of the country and following yet another audienceless showing, as the tents were being taken down and packed away for the journey to the next pitch, there was a sudden commotion among the to-ing and the fro-ing. A scream rang out, a scream of indefinable sex or origin, of such horror and unsuppressed woe that all eyes turned in the direction from whence it came.

As the boy and the girl watched, interrupted in their designated task of folding the many costumes for transportation, people about them changed their usual resigned and plodding gaits to that of the panicked, like those fleeing a fire or similar calamity.

Again came the scream, this time from elsewhere in the camp; the screamer was running about, it seemed, frantic.

"Get the nets! Get The nets!" came the cry from somewhere else, this time the voice was The Ringmaster's.

Just then The Clown ran by, screaming the terrible scream that they had heard, his face a white mask expressing just about the worst feeling a person could feel, in fact, so immense was its terror that the exact name of the emotion eluded the girl, much as she tried.

"It's in the lion's cage! The lion's cage!" wailed The Singer, and everyone dropped what they were doing and ran to see.

When they reached the lion's cage, they found The Clown's parrot inside, eyeing them all disinterestedly from the lion's painted plinth. The lion for its part was busy eyeing the parrot.

"What happened?" asked someone as they all crowded around the bars.

"It escaped!" replied another.

"How on earth could he let that happen?" asked someone else, "Doesn't he know-"

"*We all know*," interrupted yet another voice, with strange and ominous emphasis.

Just then The Clown arrived and distraught, launched himself at the bars, trying his best to climb through into the lion's cage. Others restrained him, hissing warnings of him being torn apart by the animal.

All this time the girl felt it very strange that so much fuss should be made over a parrot; a very pretty parrot it was true but only a parrot. She and her brother exchanged looks, hers: bemused, his: worried and fretful.

The Ringmaster and two others appeared at the opposite end of the cage with large nets on long poles, and proceeded to feed them through the bars in the direction of the parrot. All this time The Clown wept and wrung his hands.

Just as The Ringmaster's net was about to fall upon the bird, it took momentary flight and landed once more, just out of reach, aloof and unwilling to be caught by so rudimentary a contrivance. The little boy was just about to suggest to the crowd that perhaps the parrot might be tempted by a little birdseed, when the lion pounced.

There was a brief flapping and a blur of blue, red and yellow, and the bird was gone, crushed between the lion's massive jaws with a single bite and swallowed whole. The crowd gasped as one, The Singer fainted dead away, and falling abjectly to his knees, The Clown let out a sound that chilled the blood in the veins, a sound that would live long in the dreams of all who heard it. The boy felt sick to his stomach. The girl kept repeating under her breath that it was, after all, only a bird, yet she did so in a way that suggested that she no longer believed this. People were shaking their heads and covering their faces. The Ringmaster broke his net-pole across his knee and stormed angrily away.

A half-hearted call to get back to work was heard and people started to slowly file away from the scene. A few helped The Clown to his feet and lead him back to his wagon. When they had gone, only the children remained, looking in at the now sleeping lion.

"What do you suppose is going on?" asked the girl.

"I don't know," said the boy, "but I'm beginning to think these people might be dangerous."

"*Dangerous?*" It seemed a little too dramatic a word.

"Crazy."

"You mean a little... soft in the head?" she tried to say this with a smirk.

"Crazy," repeated her brother.

The next morning they learned that during the night The Clown had died in his sleep. Later that day, at a hastily convened funeral, they all took it in turns to pay their respects; the Ringmaster presided.

"As with feather, so with flesh," he proclaimed. An old woman nearby echoed the words solemnly, then a man did likewise, then another, then another:

"As with feather, so with flesh."

After the funeral, The Ringmaster approached the children.

"You two need a wagon of your own," he said, "Why not take The Clown's?"

Upon Waking

One morning, roughly a week after joining The Menagerie, and as the caravan made its way across the plain to who knew what destination, the brother and sister awoke in the back of The Clown's wagon to find two empty bird cages hanging by their beds.

The next morning the girl noticed two grey, nondescript birds sitting on the roof of the wagon opposite theirs. She asked her brother what kind of bird they were but he told her he didn't know. She watched them all day yet they did not move from their perch.

That night, in the hour just before dawn, something flapped and pecked against the closed shutters of their wagon and the children hugged one another in fright and willed themselves to sleep, and for morning to come.

The next day the grey birds were still there.

"Are they looking at us?" asked the boy.

"I don't know," she replied.

"I think they're looking at us."

That night, on a whim, the girl moved the two empty cages to the other side of their wagon and when the strange flapping sounds came again, they came at the shutters on the side of the wagon where the cages now hung.

The next day, the two grey birds were still there. The brother and sister watched them for a long time.

"I think they're for us," said the girl at last, "they're ours."

The Question of Escape

With every day that passed more and more grey birds appeared beside the original two, seemingly identical to one another yet strangely without identifiable markings or characteristics as to their breed or genus. At night, the flapping and pecking sounds at the shutters grew louder and more frenzied. With every new bird, a terrible feeling settled on the children and they decided to escape The Menagerie.

"It's only a matter of time before there are enough birds to peck their way into our wagon," said the girl.

"And then what?" asked the boy.

"I never want to find out," the girl replied. A plan was hastily hatched.

They would leave at night, locking the door of their wagon from the inside, climbing out of the window and fleeing back the way the caravan had come, making their way in the utter dark by feeling the tracks of the wheels in the dusty earth.

"The Ringmaster said that they never turn back. If we can get far enough away quickly enough, we'll be free," said the girl. The boy frowned.

"But I hear folks up and about at all hours of the night, what if we're seen?"

"We'll need a distraction," said the girl, "I'll sneak out and steal fuel and matches from The Fire Eater, she keeps them outside her wagon in a metal box, she daren't have them inside as it's too dangerous. Then I'll set fire to one of the bales of hay on the far side of the grand tent. While they're all running about putting it out, we'll get away." The boy agreed, and they decided that the very next night they would escape.

The Fleeing

Just as planned, under the cover of a black and starless night, the girl snuck from their wagon; from the corner of her eye she thought she saw the shadows of the now numerous grey birds watching her, but dared not look directly at them. She stole fuel and matches from the box outside The Fire Eater's wagon and crept towards the grand tent, keeping to the shadows as best she could.

The bales of hay caught fire quickly, the flames leaping almost at once onto the tent itself and the girl had to leap back lest she too be consumed in the fire.

Back at their wagon, they locked the door from the inside and gathered together what food and possessions they could carry. Already the alarm had been raised about the fire and many voices were shouting. The girl was the first to climb from the window and landing, quickly ran to the edge of the darkness before beckoning her brother to join her. She heard a strange sound, and upon turning, saw her brother's terrified face framed in the open window of the wagon, and below him, in a line on the earth between brother and sister, a row of a hundred or more of the grey birds.

"Just jump!" she told him.

"I'm frightened," he replied.

"But the fire will be out soon and our chance will be gone."

"But- The birds."

"They're only birds."

"But-" he was close to tears, "But, how will we live away from The Menagerie? What will we eat?"

"We'll make do," she replied, "we did before."

"But *the birds*."

"They're only birds," she said again, uncertainly, "and we can't stay, not after burning the grand tent. They'll know it was us, we'll be punished terribly." The boy thought for a time, then, grabbing their bundle of food, began to climb out of the window.

Just then, one of the grey birds sprang up and attacked the girl, catching its talons in her hair and pecking at her face, trying to put out her eyes. She screamed and tore it from her hair. She had just enough time to see the boy fall back into the wagon, cowering, before, with an immense flapping and squawking, the rest of the birds took flight and she was forced to run headlong and alone into the dark.

The Storm

She ran and stumbled through the night, quickly losing the wheel tracks in the dark and continued on, rudderless, onto the featureless plain, always fearing the grey birds at her back, barely able to see her hand before her face.

As dawn broke, the girl turned around to see a faint plume of smoke on the horizon, marking The Menagerie and whatever remained of the grand tent. Closer, some mile or more away, the flock of birds hung in the air, a speckled cloud shimmering in the morning light, giving chase.

She pushed on, her mouth dry and her stomach growling and empty, thinking of her brother and wondering what cover or hide she might possibly find.

Later that day she passed a small town, the familiar sight of windows boarded up and gardens hung with trip wires and animal traps. Afeared of the houses' occupants, of what they might do to her, and despite her status as a fugitive, she trod quietly, continued on and did not stop.

No sooner had she left the town than she saw in the distance ahead a terrible sandstorm, clawing up the earth and raging across the plain toward her. Looking behind her, she considered the town and beyond it the approaching shadow of grey birds. She had no other option than to try to take refuge in one of the houses.

Stepping gingerly over a lattice of tripwires hung with rusted tin cans, she approached the nearest house, expecting at any moment the crack of gunfire, perhaps the pain of a bullet wound. Every few steps she glanced about her, at the storm and then at the birds, both growing ever closer. Over another tripwire, then another. A misstep caught her foot and the tin cans rattled loudly; she froze. Nothing happened, no gunfire, no shout that trespassers would rue the day. And still the storm and the birds grew closer. Stepping over the final wires, she ran quickly to the house, found the door mercifully unlocked, and darted inside.

Meanwhile, Sisterless

 The boy had been dragged from the wagon and into a circle of sneering faces. He noticed The Singer and The Aerialists, nothing but scorn upon their faces; The Geek spat at him. He thought he saw The Juggler and The Fire Eater avert their eyes, perhaps shamed, perhaps sympathetic, but unable to speak up under the weight of the mob, the unspoken doctrine of The Menagerie. The Lion Tamer bayed for blood. The boy was beaten by The Ringmaster, his ears boxed, his nose bloodied, yet he refused to say where his sister was.
 "We took you in!" bellowed The Ringmaster, "We fed you! Kept you safe!" He held the boy roughly by his collar and spoke through his teeth into the boy's ear: "YOU WILL NEVER LEAVE US," he spat.
 The boy was thrown back into his wagon, the shutters padlocked and the door bolted. Sometime later, The Ringmaster unlocked the door, threw in a birdcage and locked the door once again. Inside the cage sat one of the non-descript grey birds, and the boy put as much distance between himself and it as he could. He stared at the bird and stared at it yet still could not identify its name or genus. And so, with nothing more to do, he stared at it and stared at it. The bird in turn stared back.
 As night fell and the interior of the wagon darkened, the boy thought he saw a change in the bird, in its shape and plumage, but could not be sure. *Was* it changing? He was sure it was, and yet that was impossible. Perhaps it was merely a trick of the failing light. Nevertheless, he took his corkscrew out of his pocket and held it tightly in his hand.

Refuge & Ingenuity

The house had been empty, as perhaps were all the other houses in the town for all she knew, but where all those people could have gone to she had no idea. As the storm raged outside, she had checked every room and every cupboard but there was no food to be found. The girl collapsed in an upstairs bedroom, so tired and so, so hungry. Her stomach moaned.

The window frames in the house rattled furiously with the wind, the doors shook and the roof made frightening cracking sounds. At any point she felt that the whole structure might be lifted up and smashed into a million pieces. With the storm's roar in her ears and thoughts of her brother's fate in her head, she fell into a troubled sleep.

She woke to an utter silence and to sunlight streaming through the boarded windows. Cautiously, she made her way downstairs, opened the door just a crack and looked out.

Clearly the flock of grey birds that had been pursuing her had reached the town shortly after the storm, for they had been thrown about by the winds, dashed against houses, and lay everywhere in small piles of feathers. At first she thought them dead but as she looked more closely, she saw the small bodies twitch and shift slightly as if merely dazed.

Leaving the house, tiptoeing across the lawn, she examined them. Next to almost every bird on the grass, there lay a small, brightly coloured egg. She was terrified, it was true, that the birds might suddenly come to their senses and rise up to peck at her, and yet the eggs looked so tasty and her stomach was so painfully empty, that she quickly darted about, gathering up the eggs and swallowing them down.

    They felt funny inside her and lay in her belly oddly, feeling like rotten grapes or like sticky stones, and she felt a little sick, yet her terrible hunger pushed her on. Soon she had eaten them all and found herself surrounded by the grounded birds, that were now beginning to flap a little more and to look around them. She looked at them, then looked back at the house, then at the traps and tripwires, and an idea came to her.

A Shadow Over The Camp

The morning after the boy's beating and imprisonment in the wagon, as tents were being packed away for the day's journey to elsewhere, a shadow fell over the camp. Eyes turned skyward yet could not, at first, discern just what had cast this enormous shade over them. People squinted and cocked their heads like cattle, shielded their eyes and strained to see.

When they did indeed begin to see just what it was up there in the sky, all hell broke loose. People dropped what they were doing and ran about, voices raised in fear and anger. The Aerialists both screamed and hugged one another, The HeShe swore, The Singer buried her head in her hands and wailed.

It was the girl they saw above them, her long hair seemingly stood on-end, but in fact plaited with stolen tripwires, those tripwires each tied to the feet of a single grey bird, hundreds in all, like a huge cloud, like a living thunderhead, carrying her through the air like some witch or magical vision; like revenge itself. She flew over the camp and the camp fled and cowered before her.

"WHERE IS MY BROTHER?" she cried out, "WHERE IS MY BROTHER?"

"He's in The Clown's wagon," answered The Juggler, "The Ringmaster locked him in The Clown's wagon." The girl descended to the wagon and as if ordered to do so, the birds immediately pecked and tore the door from its hinges.

Inside lay an opened bird cage, within it a dead Cuckoo, a corkscrew buried in its chest. Beside the cage lay her brother, also dead, though from what cause she could not see. She held him in her arms and wept, she kissed his forehead once, then, laying him gently down, turned and flew from the wagon and into the air.

The Ringmaster stood below her, cursing her name and waving his cane at her.

"We took you in!" he bellowed, "We fed you! Kept you safe! Yet you left us! Begone now, into the wilderness and starve, for there is no place for you here!"

The girl did not answer, so broken was her heart at the death of her brother, but simply held out her brother's pocketknife, cut away a handful of plaits from her hair and loosed the birds upon The Ringmaster. He was torn to shreds by the birds, who first pecked the eyes from his head with their beaks and then ripped him into ribbons with their talons. The Lion Tamer stepped forward and set her lion upon the girl, but the lion would not attack and merely lay down beneath her, rolling onto its back and showing its belly. The Lion Tamer raged and cracked her whip at the girl. The girl cut away still more plaits and loosed still more birds, and The Lion Tamer too had her eyes put out and was ripped into ribbons. The rest of the Menagerie shrank and trembled beneath the girl.

"Bring me here and now all of your cages, and in them every one of your birds!" cried the girl, "or every one of you shall have your eyes pecked out and be ripped into ribbons!"

The people did as they were told, though they were afeared of doing so. When all of their cages had been assembled before her, the girl descended and one by one opened the cages and set the birds free. With every bird that took to the sky, never to return, the crowd bellowed in fear and anguish. The girl then threw the cages to the lion, who chewed them up beyond use.

"But what will become of our birds? And what will become of us?" the people cried out, "We shall live in sorrow and uncertainty! Sorrow and uncertainty!" and they ran away across the plain, shouting "As with feather, so with flesh! As with feather, so with flesh!"

When they had all gone, the girl cut the last of the grey birds from her hair and watched them fly away. Then she walked about the camp, in and out of tents and wagons, opening boxes and food cupboards, sad for the loss of her brother and wondering just what she might do now.

Years & Quickening

    She never left the camp. She grew old there, seeing not another soul for all that time, save that of the lion, which acted as a devoted pet to her, and she never felt the need to cage it. She visited her brother's grave every day, speaking to him aloud. She slept in a different wagon every night, the lion for a pillow. Now and then a curious bird would visit but never stay very long, something in the air, some echo of what had happened there making it timorous and unsure.

    Then one day, when she had grown very old indeed, she woke and felt a strange sensation in her stomach. It was as if something lay in her belly oddly, feeling like rotten grapes or like sticky stones, and the old woman felt a little sick. She made her way into the daylight, hoping that a little fresh air might make her feel better, but it did not. The feeling inside her only grew worse. The lion watched her strangely.

    Feeling she might be sick, the old woman opened her mouth, looked up at the sky and with one enormous retch let forth an unending torrent of black birds that flew into the air, more and more, and on and on, so many that they blotted out the sun.

The End[12]

♦ Several Asides ♦

[1] *The Thing That Happened*

The thing that happened was a matter for history and history may only exist if written down. After the thing that happened, little of the written word remained, libraries burned or left derelict, empty and without use. And nothing 'official' had been written about the thing that happened itself, there simply hadn't been time.

Without documentation, without objective evidence, all that we are left with is memory, and memory is little more than a cobweb in the great scheme of things.

If, as had often been said, history was a good yardstick for the future, and when even the idea of such a future is elusive and unsure, then all anyone can be left with is the present moment, and where the next meal is coming from.

The boy and girl were told of the thing that happened by their mother, and yet perhaps it is an indication of the strange and nebulous nature of what occurred, and the difficulty in accurately describing it in a vocabulary all too used to dealing only with the usual or the everyday, that while each child heard the same story, each chose to imagine it, to conjure it in fevered dreams, in remarkably different ways.

The girl imagined the thing that happened as a rolling cloud of smoke, accumulating on the horizon and then perhaps bursting some unseen levee and advancing, jaundiced and ravenous, a dirty yellow wall of vapour, dissolving all it touched: people, animals, trees, houses.

The boy dreamed of the thing that happened as an almighty sound, like thunder, or the cracking open of the Earth itself, and yet a sound made solid stone somehow, as if the air, galvanised by the noise, became as solid granite for a mere moment, all of the air, everywhere, crushing to death in an instant all within its reach.

Neither picture of course was anything like the truth of the thing that happened, nor could it ever be. Words failed and imagery proved ridiculous in the face of it. All anyone knew was that it happened, and all that they had to show for it was that present moment, then the next, and so on.

♦

2 *The Tall Black Hat*

The hat itself, a simple, striking, beautifully crafted thing, had been made many years ago, and had passed through the hands, and indeed atop the heads, of many people. It had been made as a thing of exquisite quality, a thing of sleek blackness and lustrous sheen. In all those years, the hatband had held many a thing: feathers, folding money, photographs, playing cards and so on.

The hat may have seen better days, creases and wrinkles tainting its smooth ascent, buckling fraying the curve of its brim, and yet still it was an impressive object.

The first owner of the tall black hat had been a grand duke of some far distant principality, a round and russet gentleman of even temper and ostentatious tastes. Out riding on the very first day of the hat's purchase, the grand duke fell from his horse and broke his neck. The tall black hat tumbled from his head into the undergrowth where it lay, ridiculous in the grass, with none but the disinterested sky above it to impress, with none but a passing fox to sniff at its silken lining before darting off into the woods.

Found by a passing tradesman, the hat once again had a head to give it purpose. The man wore it that very night whilst out on a romantic boating trip with his intended. Standing to make a toast, he tipped the boat, lost balance and promptly drowned in the lake. His champagne glass sank to the bottom to the muted screams of his fiancée; the hat floated off to the opposite shore on a gentle night breeze.

A small boy fished it from the reeds some days later and set about having great larks playing dress up, until he was struck by a coach and killed that very afternoon. The boy's father sold the hat to a man who fell to a terrible and mysterious illness; this man was buried in the hat.

An opportunistic bodysnatcher (is there any other kind?) took the hat from within the man's cold coffin, and from atop the man's cold head, and within a month had been hanged -strangely enough for such a ne'er-do-well as he, for a crime he had not committed.

Another owner was lost in a terrible flood, yet another was shot while passing two men duelling, a stray bullet ricocheting and finding its mark within the cushion of his heart.

Another had fallen from a balcony, yet another suffocated, yet *another* tripped crossing train tracks; yet another choked on a peach pit.

The man driving the last wagon in the caravan had won the hat in a card game and knew nothing of its history. Perhaps it is a fact that all those who wore this beautiful hat came to a bad end because of the very fact of its wearing, or perhaps a bad end is really all that waits for any of us, whether gentleman or lady, grand duke or pauper, wearers of hats or those naked of pate?

He or she who truly knows, it seems, is not obliged to tell the likes of us.

◆

[3] *The Ringmaster*

A man once said, rightly or wrongly, that there are 3 kinds of failed actor:

#1 The actor who was successful and yet through either negligence, scandal or injury is no longer so.

#2 The actor who, while talented, and while having tried their very best, fell beneath the feet of the hoard practising that most overcrowded of professions; whether through bad luck, lack of the ability to sell themselves as a commodity, or physical and/or stylistic unfashionability.

#3 The actor who lacks sufficient talent to gain any significant level of success at all and who, upon the realisation of their failure, blames their lack on others, and so turns a bitter eye within, slowly poaching themselves as the years turn, until their innards are a stew of self-loathing, resentment and plans for punitive, if unspecified and ill-focussed, revenge.

Of these three, the last kind is the most dangerous;
The Ringmaster fell somewhere within this description.

♦

[4] *The Clown's Tale*
or
The Boy That Was Seen And Not Heard

There was once a brother and a sister who lived with their strict and cruel stepfather. Their stepfather had many rules about how the children must behave in his house, but his favourite was that they should "not speak until spoken to," a commandment whose transgression was punished swiftly with a terrible beating by cane, by slipper, or by belt.

The brother, an imaginative child, who could play by himself for hours upon end without a care, found this rule easier to follow than did his sister, who took to wearing a gag across her mouth to stop herself commenting on the wonderful weather, or on the beauty of a bird that landed in the garden, or asking questions, as intelligent children are wont to do.

One absolutely silent morning, when their stepfather did not rise at the crack of dawn as he did every day, they crept quietly up to his bedroom, and inching the door open, stepped tremulously inside. The stepfather lay dead, of heart, of stroke, of infection, of paroxysm, neither could tell, as no mark was visible on his hands or face, and even in death they feared him too much to draw back the covers and investigate further.

They both bit their lower lips and fretted, yet did not weep. They did not weep for, in truth, they were not sorry that their stepfather was dead, though they bit their lips and fretted because without his permission, how would they ever speak again?

For three long years they grew older in the house, the door to their stepfather's room nailed shut, their stepfather dead and desiccating within; dead, desiccating, and never once able to tell them that they could speak.

At night whilst they slept, the sister would scream through her gag and the brother would have very bad dreams indeed.

When venturing out for provisions, the brother would walk with his head down, not speaking to a soul (of course) and would hug the shady side of any street he happened down; because of this the townsfolk, for their part, utterly ignored him as if he weren't there at all. Sometimes the brother worried that he was a ghost, that in fact it was *he* that had died that night and not his stepfather, and all that had occurred since was some fever dream or spell that death had cast over him.

One day while out at the market, the brother, walking on the shady side of the street, saw the most beautiful girl he'd ever seen.

Her name was Maria and she was the daughter of the most successful grocer in the town. From across the square he gawped at her and for the merest moment he thought he saw her glance back at him. At that moment he fell utterly in love.

He resolved to see Maria again the next shopping day, perhaps to approach her, but how could he talk to her when he couldn't talk?

The next shopping day came and the brother practically ran into town, eschewing the shady side of the street and skidding to a halt outside Maria's father's shop. Inside he found Maria, and steeling himself, walked straight up to her, opened his mouth and...

Words dried on his lips and he cursed his dead stepfather entombed in his bedroom, he cursed him for this, a greater punishment than any cane, than any belt, than any slipper.

Maria, for her part, seemed not to even notice him, in fact began serving another customer; such an inconsequential phantom was he, so invisible to her, to everyone. He would have cried out, would have wept, would have screamed if only he could speak at all. Turning to flee his embarrassment, he tripped and fell head first into a large bag of flour. Stumbling further, he upended a table of fruit and vegetables which cascaded down onto him where he lay, every impact compounding his misery and humiliation.

He lay there, his hands and knees skinned, his abasement and shame complete, when all at once he heard behind him laughter. It was a bright, sparkling sound, the laughter of something celestial and perfect, laughter beautiful and crystalline like precious jewels cascading in sunlight. He stood and turning, saw his reflection in the bottom of a saucepan hung behind the counter. The reflection showed a flour-white face, a tomato-red nose, a strange, crooked and hopeful smile.

Then he saw that it was Maria who was laughing that wonderful laugh, and it felt to him like a declaration of love and he was hypnotised.

In fact, so hypnotised was he that he barely felt the rotten fruit, the kicks and the punches, the beating with broom handles, barely heard the shouts and the name calling, the curses and the insults, as he was run out of town and into the woods, barely felt any of them at all. As he wandered on and became utterly lost, all that he heard, and all that he craved, was to hear the beautiful crystalline laughter of Maria once more, just once more...

◆

5 *The Singer's Tale*

The Singer had once been the little girl who was sister to the little boy who later became The Clown.

Raised in that strict, silent household and having adopted the gag as a remedy as she did, it will come as no surprise that her strange predicament, and her stranger behaviour, did not lessen with the years.

When her brother failed to come back from the market that day, and indeed failed to return the day after, or the day after that, she was eventually forced out of the house and into town to find him.

The first person she met on the road into town was an old man and though she tried, she could not find it in herself to take off her gag and ask if the old man had seen her brother. The second person she met on the road was a young girl, but *still* she could not force herself to ask for help. The third person was a kind-looking woman. She waved at the kind-looking woman until her attention had been gained, and then, removing her gag, the girl attempted, after all those long years, to speak.

However, instead of words, of speech, when the girl removed her gag, all that came out was a kind of terrible, unpleasant song, shrill and grating, which hurt the ears of the kind-looking woman and forced her to flee in fright, her hands held tightly to her ears.

The girl replaced her gag and went on into town. When she got there she tried to speak to everyone she met, a merchant, a road sweeper, a baker, yet every time she removed the gag, out came that terrible song, pouring out of her, a constant stream of harsh syllable and jarring, atonal cacophony.

The townsfolk began shouting at her to stop, each of them holding their ears, then they began throwing things at her, stones, rotten fruit, anything to hand, casting her out of the town and into the forest, with warnings never again to return.

At the outskirts of the next town she came to, the girl tied the gag once more, tightly, but by now the discordant songs inside her had grown in confidence and boldness and shrieked, though muffled, through the gag until a passerby, having asked her time and again just what it was she was shrieking, and getting no comprehensible reply, wrenched the gag from her mouth, only to be greeted with the coarse and horrible sound of the songs that poured forth.

As she was pelted, beaten and driven from the second town, the gag was clawed from her hand and lost in the crowd. The girl took once more to the forest and there lived alone, only her constant and horribly unpleasant singing voice for company; alone and so terribly lonely.

After a year alone in the woods, fearing that she may never see another soul, might never fall in love, her heart finally broke and she cried and she cried. Just then, something within her changed, and as she dried her tears, she found that the songs that sprang from her were no longer shrill and terrible but were in fact beautiful and heartbreaking, resonating the pain of her own broken heart and weaving it into songs that filled the forest with beauty and sounds of wonder.

Upon realising this, the girl ran back to the nearest town, singing constantly as she went, singing and singing and singing, and was immediately welcomed, her songs stirring emotion and amazement in the hearts of all who heard her.

She was given a beautiful house to live in by the grateful townsfolk and showered with gifts. Each and every evening crowds gathered below her window to hear her wondrous voice.

After the gifts came more gifts, then more, then heartfelt and extravagant proposals of marriage and more and more, until it became clear to her that one by one the town was falling in love with her. Still she sang and still they flocked to hear her. The gifts came and the gifts came and soon, the people would not leave her alone, not for a minute, begging to hear her a little longer, a little more, arms reaching out to touch her, to paw her, to claw and hold her, such passions had her beautiful voice conjured in them.

Eventually, sleepless and driven near mad, she fled the town into the woods and from there onto the plains, and from there, well, I think we know the rest, don't we?

Whether brother and sister, Clown and Singer, gave any mark of recognition on discovering that they had both sought refuge in The Menagerie, whether they marvelled at the sheer coincidence of it all, pondered the absurd machinations of the universe, indeed whether they recognised each other at all after all those years, remains unclear.

◆

[6] *The Geek's Tale*
or
The Tale of The Feral Child

While travelling through a deep, dark forest, a family was set upon by bandits, robbed, and the mother and father killed. A boy, no more than an infant, was left by the bandits to the elements to perish. Yet he did not.

A pack of wolves discovered the child and, perhaps considering him too small to serve as any kind of meal, took his swaddling clothes in their teeth and carried him off into the trees. They raised the boy as one of their kind, taught him to hunt and to live as wolves live, with all their secrets and traditions unknown to the minds of men.

Many years later, a rich man was out hunting in the woods when he came across the wolf pack and, frightened by them, killed one and captured another, before the rest fled into the forest. It was not long before the rich man discovered that the wolf he had captured was not a wolf at all but a young man.

Astonished, he took the young man back to his grand house, and had his servants cut away the young man's long, dirty, unruly hair, had them bathe him, and had them dress him in fine clothes.

The rich man adopted the wolf-boy, and as the years went by, brought him up as his own, teaching him table manners where the wolf-boy wanted to eat only with his hands and to tear his food like an animal. He taught him to speak, where the wolf-boy wanted only to howl and to bark. He taught him to read and write, to wear clothes such as humans wore, taught him to walk upright and to be in all ways the proper son of a rich man.

In time, a neighbouring land, as neighbouring lands will, came into conflict with the rich man's land and declared war.

Great and bloody battles were staged and many lives were lost. As was right and proper, the rich man sent his adopted son off to fight the enemy; and fight he did, with great bravery, though tragically, he was killed.

The rich man was distraught and took to his bed, wracked with guilt and sorrow. And that would have been the end of the story, had the wolves not been watching.

But, so the story goes, they *were* watching, and they had been watching all those years, watching as the rich man dressed up their wolf-kin in foolish clothes, watching as his wolf-self was slowly stripped away from him, until, as a final indignity, he was sent off to fight a foolish war, a human war, which held no more sense to a wolf than did a spinning wheel to a mayfly.

Now perhaps all that really stormed the grand house that day was the rich man's guilt, but the tale told is that the wolves, in their anger, overran the rich man's servants, tore out their throats and running amok, climbed the stairs and finally found the rich man in his bed. But they did not attack him.

Instead they drove him from the grand house and out into the wilderness.

The rich man ran, for fear of the wolves, he ran and he hid. And every time he tried to make fire to warm himself the wolves chased him on, and every time he tried to seek sanctuary in a town to beg for scraps of food, to rely on that all too human kindness, they chased him on. The wolves chased him everywhere, never giving him a moment's rest until, exhausted and maddened, the rich man, now a rich man no longer, took to hunting for his food, to eating insects and wild flowers, to stealing chickens from farms and to eating them raw. And so, retreating further from his prized humanity with every day, becoming not as an animal, but lower than an animal, for the wolves in their revenge had robbed him even of the choice to be as he had been, and as he had been happy.

♦

7 *The Aerialists' Tale*

The tale of The Aerialists is, I'm afraid, practically no tale at all. Sad to say, and this will come as no surprise to some, that no extraordinary events, nor outlandish circumstance, no melodrama nor cataclysm is necessarily required for two people to be unhappy in love.

Sometimes that's just the way it is.

♦

8 *The Lion Tamer's Tale*

It is a most disheartening moment for particular keepers of animals when, thinking that the animal which they have trained and which they exhibit publicly as part of their profession is under their control, they discover that, in fact, their success or failure is, and always shall be, dependant on the whims of a beast with no more interest than use for its master's perceived, and spurious, achievement in the eyes of others.

The Lion Tamer had long since learned this lesson, a lesson that contributed significantly to her quarrelsome and aggressive nature. Perhaps it is also telling that this quarrelsome and aggressive nature had little or no effect on the demeanour of the Lion himself, who, in truth, thought her a strange and pitiful creature.

♦

9 *The Juggler's Tale*
or
Enchanted Hans

The Juggler, or Hans as was his given name, had been a master carpenter, a maker of fine furniture and carver of exquisite detail. While in business with his childhood friend Johan, his reputation as a skilled craftsman was both widely known and well deserved. It seems strangely prophetic that he was often referred to as having 'enchanted hands'; in fact he was often referred to by those who thought themselves very clever indeed, as Enchanted Hans.

While still young men, both he and Johan fell in love with the same girl, Jezreal, a local beauty. Both Hans and Johan wooed her as best they could, but Jezreal chose Hans and they were swiftly, and happily, married.

Johan was best man at their wedding but remained secretly jealous, a jealousy that drove him secretly mad as the months went on.

Hans made for his most beautiful bride a most beautiful house a mile up on the mountain overlooking the town. He carved an elaborate balcony which gave a breathtaking view of the land in which he had been born, and which had given him not only his livelihood, but also his great love, Jezreal.

Every night Hans would stand on the balcony, thanking the fates that had delivered unto him so blessed a life, and he would watch the sun go down.

A year and a day after the wedding, Hans fell ill and took to his bed, unable to work all that day. Jezreal nursed him, mopping his fevered brow and administering remedies suggested by the local apothecary. Towards the end of the day, Hans, still sick and abed, realised that for the first time since his marriage he would not be able to stand on the balcony as the sun went down and thank the fates for his good fortune. He asked Jezreal would she stand on the balcony and thank the fates for him, and she gladly agreed that she would do so in her beloved's stead.

Later, as the sun went down and Jezreal went out to give thanks to the fates as requested, Hans, from his sickbed, heard a terrible cracking sound. He leapt up and ran to the balcony just in time to see it collapse, with Jezreal standing upon it, the splintered lengths of wood falling to the rocks one mile below.

Thinking quickly, he reached out just in time to catch Jezreal's hand as she fell. And there he stood, and there she hung; he on the brink, she suspended over a terrible drop. And Hans' grip, so strong on the saw and the plane, so sure on the lathe and the chisel, in his sickness, began to slip.

Unseen on a narrow mountain path below, stood Johan, cursing himself and weeping. For it was he, driven ever madder in his jealousy, that had sawn through the supports for the balcony, thinking to send Hans to his death as the sun set, and then to claim Jezreal for his own. Unable to watch the inevitable, Johan fled, weeping, into the forest, to further delirium and derangement and to who knows what sorry end.

And Hans' grip grew weaker and weaker, and wife and husband stared at one another as it grew so, and as she finally slipped free of him, she whispered that she loved him and he watched her fall.

Down, down she went, her dress trailing after her, down she went, and he watched her all the way, watched until she became as a tumbling stone wrapped in a rag, watched her until she was little more than a speck, watched her through his tears as he knew that she was watching him through hers as she went. He watched her all the way down, closing his eyes only at the moment that she met the rocks one whole mile below.

And from that tragic day on, ignorant of Johan's part in the terrible events, Hans fell into a madness and cursed the gravity that had drawn his beloved down to her death, he cursed gravity and vowed to take his revenge upon it, to break it somehow, or to shame it somehow.

"Damn the pull of that infernal and unforgiving gravity!" he cried out to all who would listen, "that accursed edict that, birthed by the fates, did drag my beautiful Jezreal to her end. Damn the greedy inhalation of this earth! That cowardly thirst that will not show it's face but remains instead invisible in its villainy! A greed without which my love and I would now both float in the heavens above us, things of the air, rather than I, a thing fettered to lowly soil and she, a thing unjustly dashed upon the rocks by that wicked and damnable pull!"

The sorry path onward from this broken hearted carpenter to The Juggler is a path shrouded in hearsay and fable. Though some tell a story of a wandering vagabond who cursed the pull of the earth and who, one lonely night, met a strange man, or sorcerer, or diabolist, or the devil himself, at a crossroads and who, for who knows what price or trade, made a deal to kill gravity.

Though of course, as all such deals end, he was cheated and received instead only the ability to render gravity useless within his immediate vicinity, and then only up to a point; and any monies he earned with this new and startling talent, and earn them he most certainly did as he became the most astonishing juggler in the country, would simply float out of his hands and away into the sky. He remained poor, heartbroken and anchorless, a wandering juggler.

But then of course this is just a story and perhaps The Juggler's preternatural abilities were evidence, not of demonic intervention, but merely of years of painstaking practice; but when did painstaking practice ever make a good story?

♦

10 *The HeShe's Tale*

There was once born a child who was neither completely male nor completely female. Upon its birth physicians, clergymen, and those of an inquisitive, meddlesome and entitled nature, gathered around the infant's cot to peer and to pontificate.

"Is it a boy?" they asked, "Is it a girl? It must be one or the other!"

A doctor examined the baby and was astonished to discover that in actual fact it was physically half male and half female, split roughly down the middle, its left side a girl, its right a boy.

The local registrar quizzed the child's parents at length, declaring that one sex or the other must be written upon the birth certificate. Priests of all stripes and denominations argued that if the child was to be christened, or named in the eyes of any god, then it must be either boy or girl and be given a suitably male or female name.

The child's parents however simply shrugged, telling all who asked that they didn't mind which it was and that the child itself could decide if, upon aging, it found it had a mind to. This did not sit at all well with the town and they told the parents so in no uncertain terms.

The parents called the child J. Not Jason, not Jane, but just the letter J, thinking that if it so chose, the child could decide the rest of its name when it was older.

The mother and father's attitude notwithstanding, both were anxious to hear their child's first words and, in time, as it spoke more and more, to learn which sex it considered itself to be.

Once the child could articulate its feelings, it confounded all and sundry one day in school by answering a teacher (who had referred to the child as 'he') with the following phrase:

"I am not that which you say I am, I am not *he*, I am not *she*, I am we."

The child grew as the years went by into both a handsome man and a beautiful women, yet many, perhaps even most in town, never let go of their fervent claim that a person must be either one thing or another.

Despite the people's ire towards this irregularity among their number, J never once apologised nor cowered before their sneers and sharp looks, but walked tall and proud about the streets. And because of this, the ire grew, it grew into anger, and that anger grew, in time, into hate.

J was pilloried by the townsfolk, the word "Misshape!" was often thrown, and worse words still that that, words that it would not do to repeat within the pages of this tale; suffice to say that if you know a terrible word, then rest assured it was, at some point, spat at J. Nonetheless J walked tall, never once apologised nor cowered, always repeating to hateful words the phrase:

"I am not that which you say I am, I am not *he*, I am not *she*, I am we."

And then one day the police came knocking at J's door, waving an arrest warrant, two charges written in red upon it: SEDITIOUS SEDUCTION and MURDER; and J was hauled off in chains.

In the courtroom The Judge railed against the terrible crimes that J was accused of and the public gallery bayed for blood and swift conviction.

"Will the accused please state their name!" cried The Judge.

"J," said J. A murmur went round the court, the clerk and The Judge whispered furiously before The Judge spoke again.

"And is the accused male or female?"

"I am not that which you say I am," replied J, "I am not *he*, I am not *she*, I am we."

"Yes, yes," sneered The Judge, "I have heard of your he/she nonsense. But in my courtroom you will not be tried as 'we', I shall not stand for it! You shall be tried in my courtroom as a he *and* as a she."

"As two people?" asked J.

"Yes!" shouted The Judge, "as two separate people. As a man and as a woman."

"But I am not *he*, I am not *she*, I am we," said J.

"Nonsense!" cried The Judge, "Not in my courtroom you're not!"

"But I am in one body," said J calmly, "How can the law recognise two people in one body?"

"Hang the law!" bellowed The Judge, eliciting a gasp from the gallery, "The law may have its way when sentences have been given and not before. Sentences may be served as cow, goose and candlestick maker in one body for all I care, but you shall be tried how I say you will be tried and no other way! You will be tried as two people who shall be known forthwith as Man J and Woman J." And so the court went about its business and the clerk read out the following:

"Woman J, you are hereby charged that you did wantonly seduce, using your unnatural womanly charms, The Butcher, a gentleman of good standing within this community; and Man J , you are hereby charged that you did, the very next day, with malice aforethought, commit cold bloodied murder upon that same man by strangling him with your bare hands until he was dead." Another gasp ran about the court, many in the jury shook their heads solemnly.

"Do you deny carnal knowledge of The Butcher?" asked The Judge.

"I do not," replied J.

"And were you present at his death?" asked The Judge.

"I was," replied J.

And much were the accusations, and many were the raised voices, and countless were the fingers pointed and within an hour, and without any defence offered by or for J, the judge had sentenced Woman J to five years in prison for the wanton seduction, and had sentenced Man J to death for the murder. Still J remained calm.

"May I ask how Woman J is to serve her sentence of five years after Man J is put to death?" The Judge was unmoved.

"She may serve it in the grave!" he replied.

"And if I were able to prove to you that the seduction and the murder of The Butcher happened differently to the way in which it has been described here today?" The Judge guffawed loudly.

"Pah! If you could prove that to me, I hereby swear that I would eat my hat, find you innocent and give you as a gift my house, my land and all that I own!"

J then produced a love letter. The love letter was written by The Butcher confessing his love for J, and referring to J as *He who has stolen my heart and for whose strange, manly charms I yearn*. The Judge asked The Butcher's widow if the letter indeed bore her husband's handwriting; she agreed that it did.

"This letter proves that not only did I not seduce The Butcher, and not only that The Butcher seduced me, but it also proves that the *me* he was seducing was not the one that you recognise as Woman J, and who you recognise as his seducer, but instead the one you call Man J. Thus I have proven the seduction did not happen as it was described here today. The Judge shrugged.

"You are still guilty of The Butcher's murder, misshape, and you shall still hang!" he said.

J then beckoned forth a witness, a young boy.

"This is The Butcher's apprentice," said J, "a poor orphan, at night he sleeps in the butcher's shop and saw the murder take place." The boy took the witness stand and was sworn in. "Tell me, boy," said J, "did you see The Butcher's murder?"

"I did," replied the boy, "I was sleeping under the block and heard raised voices so I looked out and saw The Butcher die."

"And did you see who the raised voices belonged to?"

"I did, it was The Butcher and yourself."

"And did you hear what the raised voices were saying?"

"Yes, you said that you wished to tell The Butcher's wife of your love affair, and then The Butcher said that if you told her that he'd kill you."

"And then what happened?"

"Then The Butcher attacked you with the meat tenderiser and you strangled him."

"Aha!" interrupted The Judge, "You did it! You strangled him!" J simply held up a hand for The Judge to be quiet and to everyone's surprise, he did just that.

"And will you tell the court with which hand I strangled him?" asked J.

"Why, only with your left hand."

"Are you sure?"

"I am," said the boy, "I recall the bracelet you wear on your left wrist sparkling in the moonlight."

"That which the court will recognise as Woman J's hand," proclaimed J, "and so I have proven that neither the seduction, nor the murder happened as it was described here today and thus, judge, you must, by your own words, eat your hat, find me innocent, and give me as a gift your house, your land, and all that you own."

And so it was that despite his ranting, his raving and his screams of protestation, The Judge was forced to find J innocent, to set J free, to eat his hat and to give away his house, his land and all that he owned.

To everyone's surprise, despite The Judge's cries of "No! Wait! You're one person! I've changed my mind! Come back! Come back!" there even came a small cheer from the gallery at J's victory.

However that night, The Judge, choked with rage (and with slithers of his favourite wide-brimmed hat still stuck between his teeth) barricaded the doors to his house and burned it to the ground, hoping to catch J within it and to commit his own act of murder against the 'misshape'.

But of course J was not in the house as it burned, J instead was somewhere else entirely, in fact J never again returned to the town but moved off to pastures new and further adventures, to life, to experience both good and bad.

And so, the day of J's great victory ended, not with the immolation of a *he*, nor with the burning of a *she*, but with the escape of a *we*; and, of course, with the burning down of his own house by a foolish and angry man.

[11] *The Fire Eater's Tale*

Her daddy always said that there was none more stupid than those unafraid of fire, a nugget of wisdom that did him little good with the door locked from the outside and the flames rising.

She had stood in the garden and watched his end through the window.

They'd both taken their licks in that house, but whereas hers would heal, his would rise up on his ashes, on the winds, doubtless to come down in rain, peppering the thirsty countryside; any crops that resulted would be just about the nearest he ever came to creating anything of any damn use, she thought.

The house cracked and gave.

The road calling, she turned her back on the razing and walked on to who knew what.

◆

[12] *Epilogue*
or
Epilogues

Anyone should know that an ending is really no such thing; in fact there *is* no such thing. An ending is really just a demarcation between that which the writer wanted to impart, and the point when the writer grew tired or uninterested in imparting anything further.

Things go on, whether we're there to bear witness or not.

Perhaps, dear reader, you are interested in what became of certain players within these 'asides', perhaps in other events not fully described or detailed?

Well.

The Thing That Happened happened again. It's true to say that it waited a good hundred years or so, but it happened again; as it will always happen, and as we deserve to have it happen.

The Tall Black Hat is no more, it was pecked and shredded utterly when The Ringmaster perished. Scraps of it drifted on the winds across the plains and may be perhaps found woven into bird's nests (if indeed you can find any birds); the tiniest fragments of it may be breathed in by passersby, perhaps ingested, perhaps some of the bad luck the hat appeared to engender coming to life once more and blighting the life of those that breathed it in.

The man that once said, rightly or wrongly, that there are 3 kinds of failed actor, has since rethought his position. He now believes that all actors, regardless of achievement or circumstance, might be described as failures. Suggestions that this fresh outlook followed an unsuccessful audition on his part, can neither be confirmed nor denied.

Maria, the most beautiful girl that The Clown had ever seen, was eaten by bears.

The town that fell in love with The Singer, heartbroken at being unable to find her, all packed up their things, left the town empty and journeyed for many miles to the coast where, en masse, they walked into the sea and were never heard from again.

The deep, dark forest in which the rich man had hunted and had discovered the feral child, is now overrun by wolves, who thrive there. Every year on the anniversary of the death, in stupid human battle, of their adopted child, the wolf pack hunts and kills a single human man. I could tell you the date upon which this takes place, so that you might on that day take extra care, but then where would be the sport in that?

Unhappy love remains just as common, perhaps even more so, than happy love. Sorry.

And while they may cower from your whips and crops, animals continue to feel little more than pity and disinterest for their trainers.

Johan married, lived a long and happy life, had many children and choked to death on a fishbone at the age of a hundred and two; but his wife never loved him, she just told him that she did, and he believed her.

The Judge lived the rest of his days in abysmally mundane and misplaced anger; at the weekends he fashioned intricate models of bridges out of matchsticks, then tore them to pieces while weeping.

The site of The Fire Eater's childhood home is now an apple orchard producing just about best, juiciest apples you could ever taste; seriously, if ever you're in the area.

Actually, none of that is true. None of it. The truth is I have no idea what became of them, of *any* of them.

And nor do you.